Little Brother
PUMPKIN HEAD

by LUCIA PANZIERI

illustrated by SAMANTHA ENRIA

HOLIDAY HOUSE / NEW YORK

ONE day my mother told me that we were waiting for a little brother. The new little brother, poor guy, needed to stay awhile in my mother's tummy. I say "poor guy" because my mother started to do strange things.

She sang on the bus. I had to put myself in front of her belly to defend her and my little brother against many curious glances.

My mother said that when little ones in the tummy hear singing, they feel great joy, and when I was in her tummy, I liked to hear singing too.

Stranger than the singing on the bus, though, was that she always wanted to eat pumpkin: pumpkin soup, pumpkin dumplings, pumpkin ravioli and pumpkin pie.

My mother wanted to have a little one with hair as orange as the flesh and peel of a pumpkin. This pleased me.

Not because of the hair, but because people with orange hair have many freckles, and there's nothing I like more than a face full of freckles!

Another odd thing happened when my mother got her belly. She fell asleep as soon as she could—sometimes on the couch in Daddy's arms and sometimes on my bed while she was reading me a bedtime story.

She said it's a clever trick of nature that teaches babies-in-the-belly to sleep a lot after they are born.

One night when my mother and brother had fallen asleep on my bed, I had the dream that started all my worries. In my dream I saw my baby brother, little by little, turning into a pumpkin head—with nothing inside but seeds and pulp!

I refused to let this happen! My brother's head, even if small, needed things in it besides seeds and pulp! I had to make a rescue plan. I had to fill my brother's head with the names of plants and animals and important people.

"Don't worry, Pumpkin Head. I will tell you stories and teach you many things. And if you like, I will always be near to protect you from enemies."

First I introduced him to the sounds of our house—the water from the faucets, the oil that fried in the pan, the whistle from the teakettle and the sweet kisses that I gave Mommy.

Then winter came and my mother started to eat oranges with sugar. Even if that didn't solve the pumpkin problem, at least the vitamins from the oranges were very good for my mother and my brother.

Daddy would peel an orange with great care and arrange the sections to make a beautiful flower on the plate. I was in charge of the sugar and would make a mountain in the center of the petals.

Finally, pumpkin season ended. On the first sunny day in spring, my mother and I stood in the garden in bare feet. I could see on my mother's tummy a bump where my brother was pushing from inside. I said that maybe he wanted to come out, but my mother said he would come in the summer.

In June we went to the beach as usual. My mother had a big, beautiful belly. She rested in the sun, where Pumpkin Head's freckles would multiply.

On her belly I built a tower from shells I gathered, and I taught my little brother interesting new words: *mollusk*, *scallop*, *starfish* and *crab*.

I found a stick and drew a giant pumpkin in the sand. It was so big that all our things were inside it—us too.

Then one day Pumpkin Head was born. He left the peace
and calm of my mother's tummy, just as I did, and began to
look around with his big eyes.

He didn't have freckles or orange
hair because he was still very little.
But I could see that my brother had a
proper head.

I felt rewarded for my work. He
smiled at me and seemed to be aware of
all I had done to teach him words and
give him oranges. So we don't have to
call him Pumpkin Head anymore.

But sometimes when he's hiding during hide-and-seek, I shout, "Pumpkin Head!" And he runs to me. Because he's still too little to know the rules.

Pumpkin Head!

To my children: Chiara, Andrea and Francesco
—L. P.

Text and illustrations copyright © 2006 by Edizioni Lapis, Rome
English translation copyright © 2016 by Holiday House, Inc.
First published in Italy in 2006 as FRATELLINO ZUCCAVUOTA, and in 2014 as FRATELLINO IN ARRIVO
by Edizioni Lapis, Rome
First published in the United States of America in 2016 by Holiday House, New York
English translation by Grace Maccarone

Printed and Bound in April 2016 at Toppan Leefung, DongGuan City, China.
The artwork was created with digital tools.
www.holidayhouse.com
First American Edition
1 3 5 7 9 10 8 6 4 2

Library of Congress Cataloging-in-Publication Data

Panzieri, Lucia.
[Fratellino Zuccavuota. English]
Little Brother Pumpkin Head / by Lucia Panzieri ; illustrated by Samantha Enria ; English translation
by Grace Maccarone. — First edition.
pages cm
"First published in Italy in 2006 as Fratellino Zuccavuota""—Copyright page.
Summary: "A soon-to-be big brother has worries about his forthcoming sibling"— Provided by publisher.
ISBN 978-0-8234-3537-1 (hardcover)
[1. Babies—Fiction. 2. Pregnancy—Fiction. 3. Brothers—Fiction.] I. Enria, Samantha, illustrator. II. Maccarone,
Grace, translator. III. Title.
PZ7.P1952Li 2016
[E]—dc23
2015011049